Will the cat be found in time?

"It's gone!" shouted Mrs. Kittleman. "The bag that the cat was in is gone!"

"Maybe you put it next to a different trash can," said Alice.

"No," said Mrs. Kittleman. "This is the one."

Charlie sat down on the grass. She started to cry.

"Don't worry," said Mrs. Kittleman. "We'll find the bag." Her face lit up. "I've got it!" she said. "I know where the cat is!"

"Tell us, please!" said Alice.

"Well," said Mrs. Kittleman, "this trash wasn't empty a few minutes ago. I think the cat got picked up with the trash."

"Oh, no!" said Charlie. "That means our kitty is on its way to the town dump!"

Don't miss out on the fun!
Collect ***The Kids on the Bus***

#1 SCHOOL BUS CAT
#2 THE COOKING CLASS
#3 THE BULLY ON THE BUS
#4 THE SECRET NOTEBOOK
#5 THE FIELD DAY MIX-UP
#6 THE HAUNTED BUS

THE FIELD DAY MIX-UP

Marjorie and Andrew Sharmat

Illustrated by Meredith Johnson

HarperPaperbacks
A Division of HarperCollinsPublishers

HarperPaperbacks *A Division of* HarperCollins*Publishers*
10 East 53rd Street, New York, N.Y. 10022

Produced by Chardiet Unlimited Inc.
33 West 17th Street, New York, New York 10011.

RL 2.1 IL 007–009
First printing: July, 1991

Printed in the United States of America

HarperPaperbacks and colophon are trademarks of HarperCollins*Publishers*

10 9 8 7 6 5 4 3 2 1

THE FIELD DAY MIX-UP

CHAPTER 1

"Settle down, everybody!" said Ms. Greig to the kids in her third-grade class. "Principal Egbert is going to make an announcement to the school over the PA."

"Sounds like the whole school's in trouble," said Charlie McKee, who was sitting in the back of the room with her friends.

"Nobody's in trouble," said Clyde Fritz. "Principal Egbert is going to double our lunch recess—and you have me to thank."

"Come on, Clyde," said Max Bollen. "Why would the principal double our recess?"

"Because I dropped twenty notes into the school suggestion box asking for longer recesses," said Clyde. "I changed my handwriting each time so no one would think that only one person wrote them. I've got one of my notes with me."

Clyde pulled a crumpled-up piece of paper out of his pocket.

"Let me see that," said Marie Nast, who was sitting in front of Clyde.

Clyde handed the note to Marie.

"You're such a dummy, Clyde," said Marie. "Mr. Egbert would never fall for this. Besides, *recess* is spelled r-e-c-e-s-s. You wrote r-e-s-s-e-s-s."

"Oops," said Clyde. "Well, maybe nobody will notice."

"Get real," said Marie. "There's no way that twenty different kids would all spell *recess* wrong. Mr. Egbert will know that one person wrote all the notes. Anyway, Ms. Greig told me that the announcement is about next week's Field Day."

Everyone in class was looking forward to Field Day: an entire day in the park, running races, eating food, and playing.

Charlie was excited because she and Max were going to run the three-legged race together. That was the race where one person's left leg is tied to the other person's right leg.

"I can't wait for Field Day," said Clyde. "A whole day in the park. Just think about all the trouble we can get into!"

The PA system came on.

"Good morning, students," said the voice on the PA. "This is Principal Egbert. Today we'll be holding practices for those who'll be entering events during Field Day."

Charlie listened as Principal Egbert read the list of times for each practice. The third-grade practice was set for right after school.

Principal Egbert kept reading until all of the grades had been given their practice times.

"Good luck to all of you," he said. "And one more thing. Someone has been stuffing the school suggestion box with requests to increase lunch recess to two hours. This is not what the suggestion box is for. If this sort of thing goes on much longer, the box will be taken away. Is that understood?"

Everyone in class looked at Clyde.

Clyde slumped down in his chair. "If it had worked, I'd be a big hero right now," he muttered.

* * *

As soon as school was over, Charlie and Max ran out to the school practice area.

"Wait a minute," said Max. "One of us should run over to our bus to let Harry know that we'll be taking a different bus home."

"I'll do it," said Charlie. "You run ahead and let me know if I miss anything."

Charlie and Max split up, and Charlie ran over to the bus.

"Hi, Harry," said Charlie to the bus driver. "I just wanted to let you know that Max and I are going to a special practice for Field Day. We won't be on the bus today."

"I know all about Field Day," said Harry. "In fact, I'll be driving one of the buses to the park that day."

"Great!" said Charlie. "Maybe you'll be driving our class. Well, I have to go."

Harry smiled and winked.

"I'll see you two tomorrow," he said.

Charlie started to walk toward the practice field. Suddenly, she heard footsteps behind her. She turned around. Marie was running toward her.

"Hurry up, Charlie!" said Marie. "Practice starts in one minute." How do you expect to win any races when you're such a slowpoke?"

Charlie was starting to get mad. Marie made trouble for Charlie whenever she could. And she was always looking for a fight.

"Well, slowpoke," said Marie. "At least *I'm* going to win my race. All I need is the right partner. Guess who I'm asking?"

"I don't care," said Charlie.

"Sure you do," said Marie. "I'm asking Max Bollen to be my partner."

"You stay away from Max!" said Charlie. "He's my friend. He doesn't like you, and he won't race with you."

"Charlie," said Marie. "I didn't know you had such a temper. You must really be afraid that Max will like me more than he likes you. Well it's a free country and I can ask anyone I want. And I want to ask Max."

Charlie and Marie arrived at the practice field just as the gym teacher, Mr. Timm, was starting the warm-up exercises.

Charlie looked around the practice field, trying to find Max. But Mr. Timm pointed to a spot in the grass and told them to sit down.

"The first exercise is sit-ups," said Mr. Timm. "I want each of you to do twenty sit-ups."

Mr. Timm lay down on the grass and showed the kids how to do sit-ups. Then he blew his whistle and everyone started.

"Up! Down!" he shouted over and over.

Charlie didn't like doing sit-ups. They hurt her stomach. She grunted and groaned each time she had to sit up.

The sit-ups seemed to go on forever. Suddenly, she felt something hit her on the head.

Thump!!!

What was that? she thought as she sat up.

"Did I hit you, Charlie?" asked Marie. "It felt like my foot hit a rock. But there's no rock here, so that must've been your head."

"You did that on purpose!" cried Charlie.

Marie jumped to her feet. "I did not!" she yelled. "You were just in the way!"

"You had plenty of room for your feet," said Charlie. "You *wanted* to hit me!"

Some of the kids gathered around Charlie and Marie. "Fight! Fight! Fight!" they shouted.

Mr. Timm came over.

"All right, you two," he said. "I don't want any yelling at this practice. We're supposed to be having fun here."

"Well, I'm trying to have fun," said Marie, "but Charlie's being mean. She was yelling at me even before we reached the practice field."

"I'm going to split you two up," said Mr. Timm.

Mr. Timm led Marie to another part of the practice field. Charlie was happy to have Marie away from her.

She didn't know that Marie was being moved to where Max was exercising.

"What did you do to Charlie?" asked Max when Marie reached his area.

"I think I may have hit her by accident," said Marie. "I'm going to tell her I'm sorry. I like Charlie a lot. And I wish she could like me back."

Max stared at Marie. She looked truly sad. But Max knew he couldn't trust her. Marie was up to no good. Marie was *always* up to no good.

"Max," said Marie, "I'm looking for a partner to run with me in the three-legged race. If you want to win, you should be my partner. You and me. We'd make a great team!"

"Maybe we would," said Max, "but I already promised to run that race with Charlie."

A cold look came over Marie's face. "You can't be her partner if she's not going to race."

"What do you mean by that?" asked Max.

Marie smiled but didn't say anything.

COACH

"Tell me why you said that, Marie," Max insisted.

"No reason," said Marie. "Just forget I said it."

Max knew that something was wrong. What was Marie planning to do to Charlie?

The third-grade kids spent the rest of the afternoon practicing for the races. When it was time for the three-legged race, five pairs of kids lined up at the starting line tied to each other by their legs. Charlie and Max were teamed together, and Marie had talked Clyde Fritz into being her partner.

Mr. Timm blew the whistle, and the race began.

Charlie and Max tried to run as fast as they could, but Charlie seemed to be running faster than Max.

"This is a lot harder than it looks," said Max.

A moment later, Charlie and Max were flat on their backs. They had tripped over each other. Charlie sat up and looked around. Most of the other kids had also fallen down. Marie and Clyde were the only ones to finish the race.

"Marie's looking right at us," said Charlie. "And she's smiling. We can't let her beat us."

"Okay," said Max. "But I wish we were playing checkers instead."

Charlie and Max ran the three-legged race three more times. Each time, they got closer and closer to the finish line before falling down.

But Marie and Clyde finished every race. They looked like real winners.

"You guys are way cool!" Derek James said to them. Derek was the fastest kid in class. "With you running the three-legged race and me running the 50-yard dash, the third grade is unbeatable!"

"Yeah!!!" shouted the kids.

Charlie and Max walked away from the practice.

"We have to work at this every day this week," said Charlie.

"All right," said Max. "If that's what you want. But did I tell you that I'm also very good at chess?"

CHAPTER 3

For the rest of the week, most of the kids in the school practiced for the contests they had entered. Charlie and Max spent every afternoon practicing the three-legged race. Every day they ran the race better than they had the day before. Charlie was sure they were now good enough to win.

Marie watched them carefully. At first, Charlie wondered what Marie was thinking. But then Charlie thought, *Who cares? Not me!*

Finally, it was Field Day. When Charlie got on the school bus that morning, everyone was excited about the races.

The third graders sat together at the back.

"We're unstoppable!" said Derek James. "Mr. Timm said that we looked better in practice than any third graders he's ever seen. We're winners!"

"Winners?" said Brian Ray. The sixth-grade bully was listening to them. "You little punks really think you can win anything?"

"Yes, we do!" said Marie. "And we're going to win the school trophy this year."

"Let's get real for a moment," said Brian. "The third grade never wins anything at Field Day. The sixth grade rules. We're the *biggest* and the *baddest!*"

"Speak for yourself," said Nadine Dudley, another sixth grader. "I'm not racing. Racing messes up my hair."

"It's too bad they don't have a beauty contest for you to enter, Nadine," said Brian. "I bet you'd win the booby prize!"

The bus slowed down as it reached its last stop.

"Okay, everybody!" yelled Clyde. "What time is it?"

"It's Marvin time!" yelled Brian.

"Marvin! Marvin! Marvin!" yelled most of the kids.

Harry stopped the bus and opened the door for Marvin, a first grader.

Marvin climbed up the bus steps. His mother was right behind him. She was carrying a big blue bag.

"Good morning, Mrs. Kittleman," said Harry.

"I'm going to Field Day with Marvin," said Mrs. Kittleman. "He's still a little boy, and he might hurt himself out there."

Harry shook his head in wonder.

"What's in the bag?" growled Harry.

"Supplies," said Mrs. Kittleman. "Bandages, aspirin, cough medicine, snake-bite kit . . ."

"Snake-bite kit?" said Harry. "There are no snakes in the park."

"I believe that a person can never be too safe," said Mrs. Kittleman.

"Oh, brother," said Harry as he closed the door.

Mrs. Kittleman sat down in the front seat next to Marvin. Then she looked down at Harry's pet cat, who was sleeping in a box behind Harry's seat.

"I don't understand why the school allows that cat on the bus," she said.

Max and Charlie looked at each other. Mrs. Kittleman had been threatening for weeks to have the cat removed from the bus.

Suddenly, Marvin sneezed. "A-chew! A-chew! A-chew!"

"Marvin," said Mrs. Kittleman, "are you coming down with a cold?"

"No, Mom," said Marvin. "I feel okay."

"It must be your allergies acting up," said Mrs. Kittleman. "I'll bet you're allergic to that cat. Who knows what filth and germs that beast harbors."

Marvin sneezed a second time.

Then Mrs. Kittleman sneezed.

Soon they were both sneezing at once.

"That's it," said Mrs. Kittleman between sneezes. "That cat has got to go."

Marvin started to cry.

"I like the cat," he said. "I want it here on the bus."

"I'm sorry, Marvin," said Mrs. Kittleman. "But this is for your own good."

Charlie spoke up. "But it's such a cute little kitten. And it's our bus mascot."

"Not after today," said Mrs. Kittleman. "As soon as this bus reaches school, I'm going to complain to Principal Egbert."

CHAPTER 4

A few minutes later, the bus arrived at the school. Today, all the classes were meeting outside, next to the parking lot, before going to the park.

Dozens of kids, parents, and teachers were gathered there. Bags of supplies were piled up next to the sidewalk.

"What a mess!" said Charlie. "I hope we can find Ms. Greig's class."

"Don't worry," said Max. "We'll find them."

When Harry opened the door, Mrs. Kittleman stood up and took Marvin by the hand.

"Don't move this bus until I come back," she said to Harry. "I want Principal Egbert to see that cat with his own two eyes."

Mrs. Kittleman stomped off the bus with Marvin.

"I'm glad my mom's not like that," said Brian. "I could have turned out strange."

"We need to do something to stop Mrs. Kittleman," said Max.

"I think we should hide the cat," said Nadine. "We don't want anything to happen to it."

"I have an idea," whispered Brian. "Look out the window. See those two mean-looking dudes? They're my buddies, Rapper and Mickey. They're standing next to a pile of supply bags. All we have to do is pick the cat up while Harry's not looking and hand it out the window to one of them. They can put the cat into one of the supply bags."

"I don't like it," said Max.

"Why not?" asked Brian.

"Because it's *your* idea," said Max. "And I don't trust you."

"What's not to trust?" said Brian. "I like the cat as much as anyone. And it'll be funny to see the look on Mrs. Kittleman's face when she brings Mr. Egbert back and there's no cat here."

"Okay," said Max. "I can't think of anything else to do."

"I can't, either," said Charlie.

"You're so lucky to have me on this bus," said Brian.

Brian opened the window and called to his friends. Then Clyde sat down in the seat behind Harry and quietly picked up the cat.

Then he handed the cat back to Brian, who handed the cat out the window.

"I can't believe Harry didn't see that," said Prissy.

"Shhh! Not so loud," whispered Derek.

Harry turned around. "What didn't I see?" he asked.

"Nothing," said Derek.

"Okay," said Harry. "I didn't see you guys pick up my cat and hand it out the window. And I didn't see Brian's friends hide the cat in that bag out there."

Harry winked at the kids and turned around again.

"Now listen up, everybody," said Brian. "My buddies put the cat into the blue bag that has the winner's trophy in it. Someone has to move the cat out of the bag before the trophy is awarded."

"Our class gets to bring the trophy bag to

the park," said Charlie. "So we'll be able to keep an eye on it. Max and I will take the cat out as soon as we get to the park. Then we'll bring it back to the bus."

Brian chuckled. "Sounds like fun," he said. "I just hope you two don't mess it up."

The kids got up and walked off the bus. Charlie and Max went off to look for their classmates.

Harry started to clean the bus. He saw that Mrs. Kittleman had left her blue bag on the floor. So he picked it up and put it outside with the other bags.

A couple of minutes later, Mrs. Kittleman came back. She was alone.

"Well?" said Harry.

"There's so much confusion and noise out here that I wasn't able to locate Principal Egbert," said Mrs. Kittleman. "But when I do, I assure you that he'll agree with me. That cat won't be allowed on the bus anymore."

"We'll see about that," said Harry. "Right now, I have to get the bus ready for Field Day. I put your bag outside in the pile with the others."

Mrs. Kittleman turned and walked down the bus steps. She looked at the pile of bags that were next to the sidewalk.

Oh, my, she thought. *There are so many bags here.*

Then she saw a blue bag sticking up. *This must be mine,* she thought.

Mrs. Kittleman picked up the bag and ran off to find Marvin.

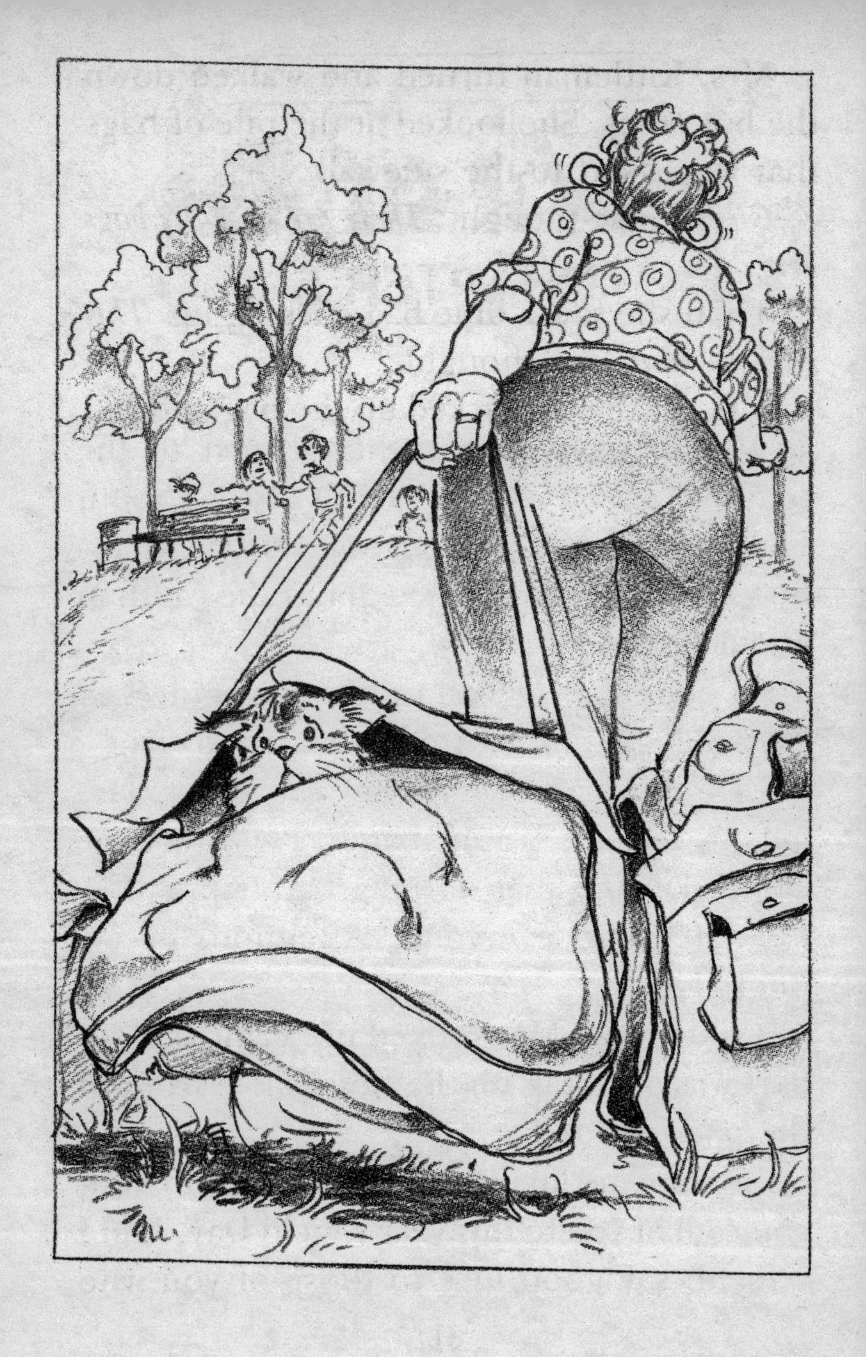

CHAPTER 5

Mrs. Greig's class gathered next to the school entrance. Everyone was excited about Field Day and about the contests. But Charlie was now more worried about the cat than about her race.

"I hope the cat's all right," she told Max. "It could get hurt sitting in that trophy bag."

"Don't worry," said Max. "Since our class gets to take the trophy bag to Field Day, we can make sure that nothing bad happens."

"Attention, everyone! Attention, everyone!"

Charlie and Max looked up. Principal Egbert was standing on the sidewalk in front of the parking lot.

"I want to take this opportunity to welcome all of you to this year's Field Day. And I want to say good luck to those of you who will be entering the contests. Now, here's a list of bus assignments for Field Day."

Charlie and Max listened as Mr. Egbert read the list. Ms. Greig's class was assigned to bus number thirteen.

"Thirteen's not a very lucky number," said Charlie.

"It is for us," said Max. "Bus thirteen is our regular bus. That means Harry will be driving us."

"Okay, everybody," said Ms. Greig to the third graders. "It's almost time for us to board our bus. As you know, we've been asked to carry some of the supplies to the park. The best part is that one of you will have the honor of carrying the bag with the trophy that will be awarded to the winning grade."

Ms. Greig smiled. "And now we're going to find out who that lucky person is. I've placed each of your names in a hat. Prissy, please come up and draw a name out of the hat."

Prissy put her hand in the hat and pulled out a name.

"And the winner is . . . Alice Wiczer!" said Prissy.

"Yeah!!!" shouted Alice.

"Yeah!!!" shouted Charlie. She was glad that Alice would be carrying the cat to the park. If someone else found the cat in the bag, there might be trouble.

"Now remember, Alice," said Ms. Greig. "No one is allowed to see the trophy until it's awarded to the winning grade. Absolutely no one!"

"Uh-oh," Max whispered to Charlie. "The trophy bag is supposed to stay closed all day. That means that the cat is stuck in there until the end of the races."

"It can't stay in there all day," said Charlie.

"You're right," said Max. "What if the cat pees on the trophy—or worse?!"

"Max, think of something!" Charlie said.

The kids in Ms. Greig's class picked up the supply bags and boarded Harry's bus. Alice carried the blue trophy bag to the back of the bus and sat down. A small group of kids gathered around her.

Ms. Greig sat up front, in back of Harry.

Charlie and Max sat by themselves so they could think of a plan.

"Any ideas?" asked Charlie.

"Sure," said Max. "When we get to the park, we open that bag when no one is looking. Then we sneak the cat back onto the bus."

"Then what?" asked Charlie.

"We put the cat into another bag and get Harry to hide it for the ride home," said Max.

"It might work if we get the other kids on the bus to help us," said Max. "When we get to the park, we could ask them to help block the view while I open the trophy bag and take out the cat. We could do it the minute we reach the park."

"But right now we have to tell Alice that the cat's in her bag," said Charlie.

"Not now," said Max. "We have to wait until she's alone."

A few minutes later, the bus pulled into the park. Many other buses had already arrived.

The first and second graders were being taken to the playground area. They were too young to compete in the contests.

Harry opened the door, and Ms. Greig led her class off the bus.

"The third grade rules!" shouted Clyde.

"The third grade stinks!" yelled Brian Ray from across the field. "The *sixth* grade rules!"

Suddenly the whole sixth grade started shouting.

"THE SIXTH GRADE RULES!!! THE SIXTH GRADE RULES!!! THE SIXTH GRADE RULES!!!"

Then everyone was yelling at once. Principal Egbert tried to quiet the kids down, but nobody heard him over all the noise.

The yelling went on and on.

"This is our chance to tell the other kids about our plan," said Charlie.

Charlie walked over to Prissy and tapped her on the shoulder.

"We have to sneak the cat out of the trophy bag before the trophy is awarded," said Charlie. "We have a plan, but we need your help."

"I'm sorry," said Prissy. "But every teacher in school is at Field Day. The principal is here, and mean old Miss Peck is here, and lots of parents are here. We'd get caught for sure."

"But we need your help, Prissy," said Charlie.

"I'd like to help you, Charlie," said Prissy, "but I'm afraid of getting in trouble."

Prissy bolted away.

Charlie walked over to Marie. She didn't want to ask Marie for help. But Marie liked Harry's cat, and Charlie was ready to accept help from anywhere she could find it.

Marie was shouting along with the other

kids. Charlie stood right in front of her, but Marie pretended she didn't see her. She kept right on shouting. Charlie waved her hands back and forth.

Marie made a face. "What do you want?" she asked.

Charlie told Marie about her plan.

"Why should I help *you?*" asked Marie.

"This isn't just for me," said Charlie. "That cat is our bus mascot. If the cat is discovered, Harry could be in big trouble. He could even lose his job."

"Then tell Harry to go get his cat," said Marie. "I've got better things to do."

"Fine!" shouted Charlie. "I don't want your help anyway!"

Charlie stormed away from Marie.

While Charlie was asking Prissy and Marie for help, Max went over to Clyde.

"Clyde," said Max, "we have to get the cat out of the trophy bag. If we don't, Alice will open the bag, and the cat will jump out instead."

"What a riot!" said Clyde. "That'll be the funniest thing that ever happened on Field Day! Thanks for telling me about this. I'll make sure I'm in the front row when the cat —I mean, the trophy—is awarded."

"Well, I guess I can forget about Clyde," Max said to himself as he walked over to Derek.

Derek was yelling louder than anyone else.

"THIRD GRADE RULES!!! THIRD GRADE RULES!!!"

"DEREK!!!" Max yelled. "I HAVE TO TELL YOU SOMETHING!!!"

"NOT NOW!!!" shouted Derek. "I'M CHEERING FOR THE THIRD GRADE!!!"

"BUT THIS IS IMPORTANT!!!" shouted Max.

"SO IS THIS!!!" yelled Derek. "TELL ME LATER!!!"

Max walked back to Charlie. They would have to rescue the cat themselves.

After all the shouting had stopped, the kids took the supplies out to the park. Three separate areas had been set up: a racing area, a cooking area, and a game area.

Charlie and Max followed Alice down to the cooking area. They watched Alice put the trophy bag down onto a picnic table.

"We can't wait," said Max. "We have to get the cat out as soon as we can. Now's the time to tell Alice that she has a cat in her trophy bag."

Charlie and Max walked over to Alice.

"Have you seen the trophy yet?" asked Charlie.

"No," said Alice. "I'm not allowed to look inside the bag. But I've heard that this year's trophy is the best ever."

"That's right," said Max. "It's the first trophy in the school's history that can chase mice and purr."

"What do you mean by that?" asked Alice.

"I mean that our school bus cat is hidden in the trophy bag. It's in there right now."

Alice stared at Max. "You're joking," she said. "I know you are. And it's not funny!"

"It's no joke," said Charlie. "We've got to open the bag when nobody's looking and take the cat out."

"Well, nobody's looking now," said Alice. "Take the cat out! Get it out of the trophy bag!"

"Okay," said Max. "But both of you have to stand in front of me so no one can see when I take the cat out."

Max crept over to the picnic table. Charlie and Alice followed after him.

Max crawled under the table and pulled the bag down from the top.

"Max Bollen!" yelled Ms. Greig. "Let go of that bag this instant!"

Max stood up.

"Nobody's allowed to see the trophy until the presentation ceremony," said Ms. Greig.

"I want you and Charlie to come over here and help me set some tables."

"Now what am I going to do?" asked Alice. "You guys are my friends, and I love that cat even though I don't ride the bus with it. But you've got to get that cat out of the trophy bag."

Alice walked away.

"Are you coming?" Ms. Greig called again.

Charlie and Max started to set tables together.

"I've got a bad feeling about this," said Charlie in a low voice to Max. "What if something awful happens to the cat in that bag? If it does, it'll be our fault."

"I've got a bad feeling, too," said Max. "When I picked up the bag a minute ago, I didn't feel anything like a trophy. And I didn't feel the cat, either."

"Are you sure?" asked Charlie.

"Not totally," said Max. "I only had the bag for an instant. But I think Harry's cat is gone."

CHAPTER 8

While the older grades were setting up for their contests and picnic, the first- and second-grade kids were unloading their own picnic supplies in the playground area. Some of the bags were too heavy for them to carry. Their teachers and parents were helping with those.

Marvin Kittleman was with his best friend, Aaron Fong, who was also in the first grade.

"Can we run ahead, Mom?" asked Marvin.

"Okay," said Mrs. Kittleman. "But don't run too fast. You don't want to strain yourselves."

Marvin and Aaron ran over to the swings.

Mrs. Kittleman was helping bring bags over to the playground. When she was finished, she picked up her own blue bag and walked over toward the swings.

This is a wonderful day, she thought. *The sun is out. The kids are having fun. And—*

"Meow!"

Mrs. Kittleman froze.

What was that? she asked herself. *It sounded like a cat!*

"MEOW!"

Mrs. Kittleman turned around. "Who did that?" she shrieked.

The kids looked at her, but no one said a word.

"Who made those cat noises?" she shouted.

Suddenly, she felt something move in her bag. Mrs. Kittleman quickly set down the bag on the ground.

"Meow!"

"This is just terrible!" she said. "Someone's put a horrible, filthy cat in my Marvin's supply bag."

Mrs. Kittleman started to sneeze. "A-chew! A-chew! A-chew!"

I can't even be near this bag, she thought. *I'll just leave it here and get Principal Egbert. When he finds out about this, he'll be as angry as I am.*

Mrs. Kittleman put the bag down next to a

trash barrel and went to look for Principal Egbert.

Every year, the third-grade classes started Field Day by singing songs to the older grades. As soon as Ms. Greig's class finished setting up their supplies, they gathered with the other third graders in front of the buses. The older kids sat down in front of them.

Charlie didn't want to sing. She wanted to stay at the picnic area and open the trophy bag. She had to find out where the cat was.

What if the cat is gone? she asked herself. *Where will I look?*

But it was time to start the singing. Charlie didn't want to be up front, so she found a place at the back of the group.

Mr. Egbert walked over to the front of the third-grade group.

"Attention, everybody!" he boomed. "Once again, it's time to start our yearly Field Day Games. For those of you in the sixth grade, this is the last time you'll be competing in these contests. Those of you in the third grade will be competing for the first time."

"Third grade rules!" yelled Clyde.

"Be quiet, Clyde," whispered some of the kids.

"Each year," continued Mr. Egbert, "the third-grade class starts the games by singing three songs. When the songs are over, the games will begin."

The third graders began to sing. Charlie sang along with the rest of the kids. Then she noticed that Marie was standing right next to her.

I didn't even see her, Charlie thought. *But I know she's here for a reason—and I don't like it.*

Charlie looked at Marie. Marie looked at Charlie. Charlie was sure that something bad was about to happen.

TRAS

The third-grade class sang the first two songs. Charlie eyed Marie, waiting for her to start trouble. But Marie just stood in place.

Then the school "fight" song started.

Charlie started to sing as loud as she could.

Fight on, mighty Bull Dogs!
Fight on, green and white!
Fight on, mighty Bull Dogs!
Show our spirit day and—

"OOWWCCCHH!" screamed Charlie. For a moment, she could think of nothing but the pain that shot through her right foot.

Then she figured out what had happened. Marie had stomped on her foot.

Charlie glared at Marie. "I know you did that on purpose! You're afraid I'm going to beat you in the race! But I'm not afraid of you. Max and I will win—that's a promise!"

Marie smiled at Charlie. "We'll see," she said.

Charlie hopped on one foot and held back tears.

"Here comes Ms. Greig," said Charlie. "I'm telling her what you did. There's nothing you can do to stop me. You'll be tossed out of the race for cheating."

"You won't tell her that," said Marie. "If you do, I'll tell her that you put a cat in the trophy bag. I'll also tell Mr. Egbert that Harry's been keeping the cat on our bus all year."

"You wouldn't do that!" said Charlie.

"That depends on what you say, Charlie," said Marie. "But if you tell on me, it's all over for Harry's kitty."

Charlie gave Marie a cold stare. She felt totally helpless.

Ms. Greig came over.

"What's going on here?" she asked.

Charlie wanted to tell on Marie. But she knew what would happen if she did.

"What's going on here?" repeated Ms. Greig.

"Nothing," said Charlie.

"Then what's all the shouting about?" asked Ms. Greig.

"I *thought* that Marie stepped on my foot on purpose," said Charlie. "But I was wrong."

"Well, it's not very nice to accuse someone of something like that, Charlie," said Ms. Greig. "I think you should say you're sorry to Marie."

"I'm sorry, Marie," said Charlie.

Marie grinned. "Thank you, Charlie," she said. "I won't hold this against you."

Charlie wanted to cry. Marie had made her look stupid. And her foot was hurting. And Harry's cat was still stuck in the trophy bag—maybe.

It was time for the races to begin. Charlie limped over to the field along with Max and the other students. Her foot still hurt, and she wondered if she'd be able to run her race.

Charlie saw Alice sitting by the trophy bag. Alice was petting the bag and talking to it.

"Look at Alice," Charlie said to Max. "She's talking to the cat. Someone's going to see her and get suspicious."

"Suspicious?" asked Max. "No one would ever think there's a cat in the trophy bag. They'll just think that Alice is a little strange."

"We have to get to that bag," said Charlie. "But how?"

"We may get a chance very soon," said Max. "The first event is the broad jump. While everybody's watching the contest, we'll open the bag."

The broad jump event began. Charlie and Max told Alice about their new plan. Alice picked up the trophy bag and walked to a quiet area away from the other students. Nobody seemed to notice.

A moment later, Charlie and Max sat down next to her.

"So far, so good," said Charlie.

"Good," said Max. "Now, Alice, you wait until they blow the whistle for the next runner to start. Open the bag at that instant."

Alice waited for the whistle. When it came, she opened the bag and reached inside.

"Well?" said Charlie.

"This is weird," said Alice. "There's no cat in here, and . . . there's no trophy."

"No trophy?" said Max. "There's got to be a trophy in there."

"There isn't," said Alice. "All I see is a bunch of bandages, pills, a sweatshirt, and a snake-bite kit."

"A snake-bite kit?" said Charlie. "I don't get it."

"I do," said Max. "This isn't the trophy bag. This is Mrs. Kittleman's bag. She brought it on the bus this morning."

Max pulled out the sweatshirt. The name tag on the sweatshirt read: MARVIN KITTLEMAN.

"It says 'Marvin Kittleman.'!" said Max. "Somehow the two bags got switched."

"That means Mrs. Kittleman has the trophy bag—with the cat in it," said Charlie.

"Right," said Max.

"But Mrs. Kittleman wants to get rid of Harry's cat!" cried Charlie.

"We have to stop her," said Max. "But we can't do it ourselves. I'm going to ask Ms. Greig to help us."

Max ran over to Ms. Greig.

"I feel like running into the woods and hiding from the world," said Charlie. "But with my luck, I'd get poison ivy."

Just then, Marie walked up to Charlie and Alice. "I just came over to wish you luck in the race, Charlie," she said. She smiled, but it was a mean smile.

Just then, Max brought Ms. Greig back to where Charlie, Alice, and Marie were standing.

"It seems that we have to find Mrs. Kittleman," said Ms. Greig, "and trade bags with her."

"But what if she's already seen the cat?" asked Charlie. "She'll go straight to Principal Egbert."

"There's nothing we can do about that," said Ms. Greig. "But so far, I haven't seen any parent with a cat talking to Mr. Egbert. So there still might be time to reach her."

Marie looked confused. "What are you guys talking about?" she asked.

"The bag Mrs. Kittleman brought on the bus this morning got switched with the trophy bag," said Max. "And since the cat's in the trophy bag, one of us has to find Mrs. Kittleman and trade bags with her."

"I'll go," said Alice. "I'm supposed to be responsible for the trophy bag."

"Okay," said Ms. Greig. "But someone who knows what Mrs. Kittleman looks like should go with you."

"I think Charlie should go," said Marie.

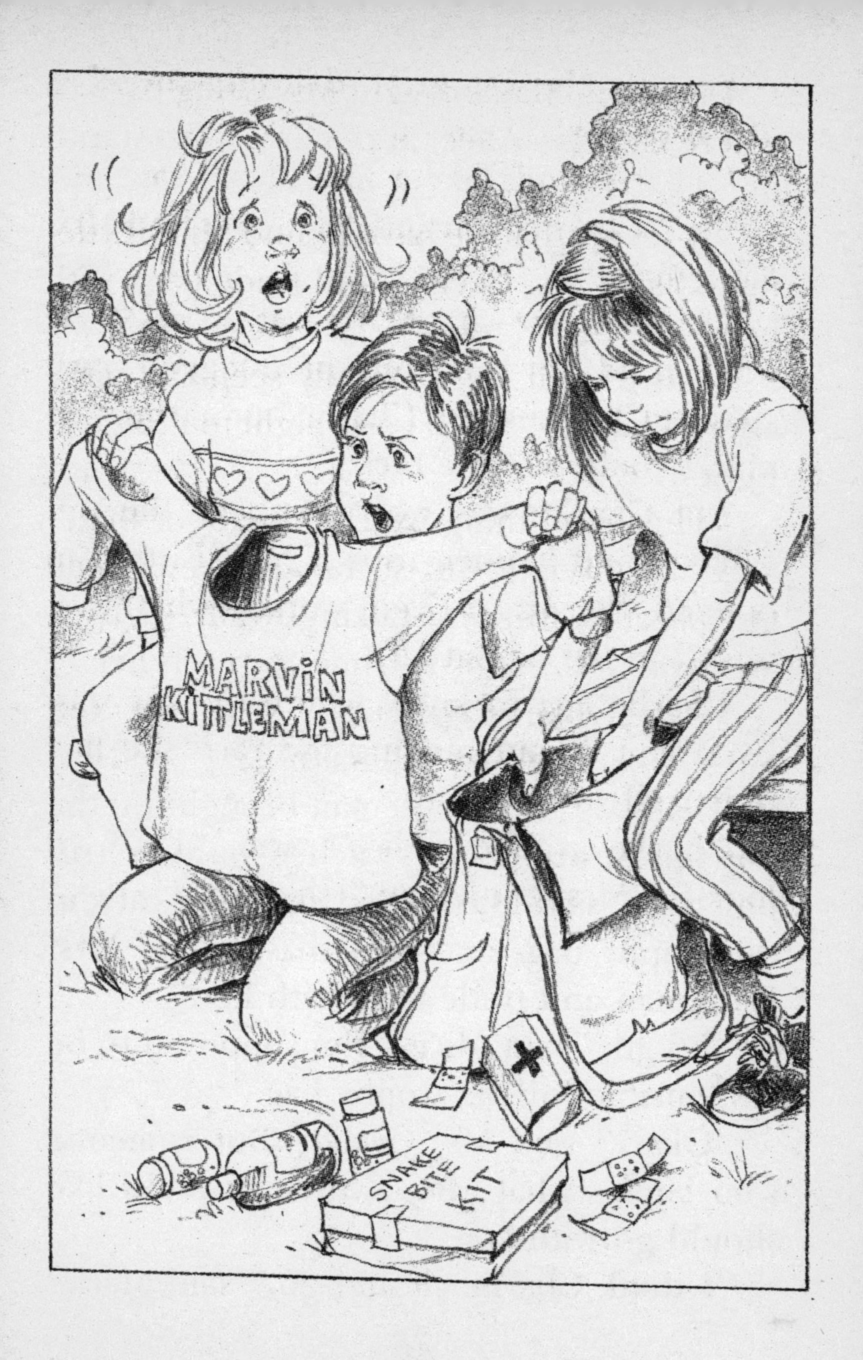
MARVIN
KITTLEMAN
SNAKE
BITE
KIT

"She likes the cat more than anyone else. She'll take good care of it."

"That sounds like a fine idea," said Ms. Greig. "Charlie, you and Alice help find Mrs. Kittleman."

Charlie knew what Marie was up to. Marie was afraid to run the three-legged race against Charlie. With Charlie out of the way, Marie could win the race.

But Charlie was worried about the cat. What would happen to it if Mrs. Kittleman opened the bag? Even worse—what if it wasn't in the bag at all?

Charlie *had* to know where the cat was. Even if it meant missing the race she had practiced so hard for.

Charlie grabbed Alice's arm. "Let's go look for Mrs. Kittleman," she said.

Charlie and Alice ran to the playground where the first and second graders were. Charlie was clutching Mrs. Kittleman's bag. "Hurry up, Alice!" she said. "We may be too late already."

"I'm going as fast as I can," said Alice.

"Look!" said Charlie. "There's Mrs. Kittleman."

"But she's not carrying a bag," said Alice. "And she's not carrying the kitty."

Charlie and Alice rushed up to Mrs. Kittleman.

"Hi, Mrs. Kittleman," said Charlie. "My name is Charlie, and I ride on the same bus as Marvin. This is my friend Alice."

Charlie was feeling nervous, but she tried to smile at Mrs. Kittleman. "We think that your bag and our trophy bag got mixed up somehow," she said. She handed Mrs. Kittleman's bag to her.

"Do you have our trophy bag?" asked Charlie.

"I *had* a big blue bag," said Mrs. Kittleman. "And there was a cat inside it. I'm sure it was that filthy animal that Harry keeps on the bus. Just the thought of that thing makes me want to—A-chew! A-chew! A-chew!"

"But what about the trophy?" asked Alice.

"I didn't see it in the bag," said Mrs. Kittleman. "But I wasn't looking for it, either."

"We need to get the bag as soon as we can," said Charlie.

"Well," said Mrs. Kittleman. "I was on my way to report this to Principal Egbert. The school bus is for children. It's not for animals."

"But we love the cat," said Charlie.

"Let me get this straight," said Mrs. Kittleman. "Are you saying that you want that germy, hairy, sneeze-provoking creature on your bus every day?"

"Right," said Charlie.

Mrs. Kittleman frowned. "Marvin is allergic to something, and I suspect it's the cat."

"It could be broccoli," said Alice.

"Broccoli?" said Mrs. Kittleman.

"Just a guess," said Alice.

"I know Marvin would be very upset if anything happened to the cat," said Charlie.

Mrs. Kittleman kept frowning. "I want to do the right thing, you know. If all you children like this cat so much—"

"We do! We do!" said Charlie.

Mrs. Kittleman smiled at Charlie. "Then I won't report Harry," she said. "At least not for a while. I'm going to take Marvin off broccoli and see if he stops sneezing."

"If he doesn't, get rid of Brussels sprouts," said Alice.

"Brussels sprouts?"

"Yes. Actually, I have a long list of sneeze suspects," said Alice. "Wool, snails, tulips—"

"One at a time," said Mrs. Kittleman. "Meanwhile, I won't make trouble about the cat. Now, let's go find the trophy bag."

Charlie felt happy as she followed Mrs. Kittleman. But she didn't stay happy for long.

CHAPTER 12

"It's gone!" shouted Mrs. Kittleman. "The bag is gone!"

"Are you sure you left it here?" asked Alice.

"Yes," said Mrs. Kittleman. "I put it down right next to this trash can. Somebody's taken it."

"Maybe you put it next to a different trash can," said Alice.

"No," said Mrs. Kittleman. "This is the one."

Charlie sat down on the grass. She started to cry.

"Don't worry," said Mrs. Kittleman. "We'll find the bag. If only I could figure out where to start looking!"

Mrs. Kittleman scratched her head. Suddenly, her face lit up. "I've got it!" she said. "I know where the cat is!"

"Tell us, please!" said Alice.

"Well," said Mrs. Kittleman, "this trash can is empty. It wasn't empty a few minutes ago. I think the cat got picked up with the trash."

"Oh, no!" said Charlie. "That means our kitty is on its way to the town dump!"

"Yuck!" said Alice. "Locked in a garbage truck with all that smelly garbage!"

"That's not all," said Charlie. "The cat could get crushed with all that garbage piled on top of the bag!"

"We have to get to the dump," said Mrs. Kittleman. "But it's too far to walk."

"Then let's get Harry to drive us," said Charlie.

Charlie, Alice, and Mrs. Kittleman ran to where the buses were parked.

"Harry!" shrieked Mrs. Kittleman. "Help us, please! We have to go to the dump!"

Harry looked at Charlie. "The dump? Is this for real?" he asked.

"Yes," said Charlie. "The bag with the cat in it was left next to a trash can. Now it's gone. We think it was taken away with the garbage."

"Oh, no!" shouted Harry. "Everyone get into your seats and hold on tight. We've got to chase down a garbage truck!"

Harry started up the engine.

VROOOMMM!!!

The bus zoomed out of the parking lot and onto the road. Charlie could hear the tires screeching.

"Wow!" said Alice. "This old tank can really move!"

Charlie looked out the front window. The road ahead was full of cars. "What'll we do now?" she asked. "We'll never catch up with all this traffic in the way."

"Little lady," said Harry, "you forget that you're riding with a master driver. The old heap and I can do anything."

Harry pointed to a black box on the floor.

"Open the box," he said to Charlie. "And hand me what's inside."

Charlie opened the box and looked. "What is this thing?" she asked.

"It's a siren," said Harry. "I never use it. But this is an emergency."

Harry reached out and attached the siren to the outside of the bus. Then he flicked a switch. The siren made a loud howling noise. Mrs. Kittleman covered her ears.

One by one, all the cars on the road pulled over to the side.

"It's smooth sailing now," said Harry. "And there's not a garbage truck in the country that can outrun this old heap!"

"We're getting some strange looks from the other drivers," said Alice. "I think they're expecting a police car, not a school bus."

After the traffic thinned out, Harry turned off the siren. He handed it to Charlie.

"Look!" said Alice. "There's the garbage truck up ahead. Honk the horn and hope it stops."

Harry honked the horn, but the garbage truck kept going. He honked a second time, but the truck still didn't stop.

"I'm going to pass the truck," said Harry. "Charlie, I want you to go to one of the windows, open it up, and motion the driver to pull off to the side."

Charlie opened a window and started waving at the driver. The driver smiled and waved back at Charlie.

"It's not working!" said Charlie. "What can we do to make him stop?"

"I'll pull up in front of the truck," said Harry. "Everybody go to the back of the bus and point the driver to the side of the road."

Charlie, Alice, and Mrs. Kittleman ran to the back window and started waving the truck driver over. He pulled over to the side of the road and stopped the truck. Harry stopped the bus right in front of it.

He opened the door, and everyone ran over to the garbage truck.

"What's going on here?" said the truck driver.

"We're looking for a blue bag left in the park. It has a cat in it," Harry said. "We think the bag got mixed into the trash."

"This is your lucky day," said the garbage-truck driver. He opened his door and picked up the cat, which was sitting quietly next to him.

"Yeah!" shouted Charlie.

"Who gets it?" said the driver.

"I do! I do!" said Charlie.

The driver handed the cat to Charlie. She gave the cat a big hug. It purred in her arms.

"How did you know there was a cat in the bag?" asked Harry.

"Did you ever hear of garbage that meowed?" asked the driver.

"Well, I just want to say thanks," said Harry.

"No problem," said the driver. "I'm glad you showed up. I didn't know what I was going to do with the little fellow."

"But what about the bag the cat was in?" asked Alice. "The trophy is still in the bag!"

"One trophy coming up," said the driver as he held up the blue bag. "It's in here," he said.

Alice grabbed the bag. Charlie held the cat.

"Thank you, thank you!" they said to the driver.

"Come on. We'd better get back," said Harry. "People are going to think something has happened to us."

"And I have to race against Marie," said Charlie. "I hope I'm not too late."

CHAPTER 13

Harry drove Charlie, Alice, and Mrs. Kittleman back to the park. As they got off of the bus, Derek James ran up to them.

"I heard about the switched bags," he said. "Where's the trophy, and where's the cat?"

"The trophy's in the blue bag," Alice said. Then she whispered, "and the cat's back on the bus. It seems really happy to be there."

"Hey, everybody!" Derek yelled. "Alice and Charlie found the trophy!"

A moment later, a big crowd of kids, parents, and teachers gathered around Charlie, Alice, and Mrs. Kittleman.

Principal Egbert walked through the crowd and stood next to Alice and Charlie.

"Ms. Greig told me about the trophy bag being switched. But when you disappeared, I became concerned. What happened to you?"

Alice spoke up. "The cat—" she began. "I mean, the trophy was taken away in a garbage truck by mistake. Harry drove us toward the city dump. We caught up to the garbage truck on the way."

"So the trophy was in with all the garbage?" said Principal Egbert.

"No," said Alice. "The trophy was up front with the driver."

"That's very strange," said Principal Egbert. "Why would the driver know to keep the trophy bag up front with him? That doesn't sound right to me."

Alice gulped. "Because . . . because . . . because . . ."

"Because there was also a cat in the bag!" Harry said from the bus. "I bring my pet cat on the bus with me. The cat keeps me company, and the kids are very fond of it."

Harry took a deep breath and went on. "The cat was put in the trophy bag by mistake. The garbage truck driver found the cat. And the trophy just happened to be in the bag with the cat."

Principal Egbert looked at Harry.

"Hmmm . . . I don't know about a cat on a bus," he said. "But your cat kept the trophy from being thrown in with the garbage. In a way, the cat's kind of a hero."

"Yeah!!!" yelled some of the kids.

"I'll have to talk to the school board about your cat riding on the bus," said Principal Egbert. "But if no one objects, I'll ask that it be approved."

Harry looked at Mrs. Kittleman. "Mrs. Kittleman here thinks that—"

Mrs. Kittleman interrupted Harry. "I think that the cat can stay on the bus. By the way, have you ever heard that broccoli causes sneezing?"

"Broccoli?" Harry cocked his head. "Uh—I'll keep all broccoli off the bus, just in case," he said. Then he raised his arms. "The cat stays!"

"Yeah!!!" yelled the kids again.

"I'd also like to hear three cheers for Alice, Charlie, and Mrs. Kittleman," said Principal Egbert.

Everyone cheered as loud as they could—everyone but Marie. She just stood silently in place.

But as soon as the cheering stopped, she ran up to Charlie.

"I have something to show you, Charlie," she said. She pulled a ribbon out of her pocket. Printed on the ribbon were the words: FIRST PLACE.

"I won this while you were gone," Marie said.

"I'm very happy for Clyde," said Charlie. "He should win a medal just for running in the race with you."

Marie grinned. "Clyde didn't run with me," she said. "I ran with Max!"

"I don't believe you!" said Charlie. "Clyde was your partner, not Max!"

"Clyde hurt his foot before the race," said Marie. "I needed a partner. And since you were gone, Max needed a partner."

"You're a slimy snake, Marie," said Charlie. "I'll bet you had something to do with Clyde's foot being hurt. Didn't you?"

"You're a sore loser, Charlie," said Marie.

Marie turned and walked away.

CHAPTER 14

As soon as all the races were over, it was time to award the trophy. The sixth grade had won most of the contests. The sixth grade had been winning at Field Day for as long as anyone could remember. The big surprise this year was that the third grade had finished second. The third grade had never finished second before.

Alice unwrapped the trophy. It was given to the captain of the sixth-grade team. As the trophy was presented, Brian Ray yelled out, *"Sixth grade rules!"* The sixth graders all started shouting at once. Not even Principal Egbert could calm them down.

Charlie wasn't listening to all the shouting. She was too mad—mad at Marie for being so mean, and mad at Max for being Marie's racing partner.

Max tried to explain that he had run the

race to help the third grade and not Marie. But Charlie didn't care.

While the sixth graders cheered, Max walked over to Ms. Greig. She bent down as Max whispered something in her ear. Then Ms. Greig rushed over to Principal Egbert and Mr. Timm. She started talking to them.

Suddenly, Principal Egbert climbed up onto a picnic table and asked the sixth graders to calm down.

"It has come to my attention that one of the students who rescued the trophy didn't even get a chance to run in her race. Charlie, I'd like for you and your partner Max to come up and run the three-legged race together."

Charlie walked over to Max. "You set this up, didn't you, Max?" she said.

"Sure did," said Max. "And wait till you see who we're running against."

Principal Egbert looked out at the students.

"I'm looking for Marie Nast," he said. "Marie is our other champion at the three-legged race. I'd like her to choose a partner and race against Charlie and Max."

Marie ran over to Clyde. "I want you to be my partner, Clyde. You're really good at this kind of race."

"Keep away from me, Marie," said Clyde. "You stepped on my foot. You're dangerous."

"I didn't do it on purpose, Clyde," said Marie.

"But my left foot is still really hurting," said Clyde.

Marie growled. "If you don't run with me, your right foot is going to hurt even more than your left foot."

Clyde and Marie went to the starting line.

Charlie and Max were already there, waiting.

"How's your foot, Charlie?" asked Max.

"It still hurts," said Charlie. "But I think I can run on it."

Mr. Timm tied Charlie's and Max's legs together. Then he tied Marie's and Clyde's legs.

Marie looked at Charlie. "I've beaten

you every time, Charlie," she said. "Now I'm going to beat you in front of the whole school."

"Not this time," said Charlie. "This time *you're* the one who's going to lose."

"On your mark!" yelled Mr. Timm. "Get set . . . GO!"

Charlie's foot did hurt when she hopped on it. But she couldn't let Marie win.

Charlie wasn't the only one with an aching foot. Clyde could barely run at all.

"Faster, you dummy!" Marie screamed. "Faster!"

"I can't go any faster!" said Clyde. "Limping is my fastest speed!"

"We're winning!" said Max. "They're falling behind!"

"That's nice," said Charlie. "But my foot really hurts."

"You've got to go faster!" Marie screamed to Clyde. "We're losing to Charlie!"

"My foot stings," said Clyde. "I can't go any further."

Suddenly, Clyde dropped to the ground. Marie tried to stay on her feet, but her leg was tied to Clyde's leg. She ended up down on the ground next to him.

"Get up!!" she ordered. "Get up!!"

"I'm finished," said Clyde. "I'm staying right here forever."

"You dummy!" snapped Marie. "You've ruined everything!"

Meanwhile, Max was almost carrying Charlie. They were going forward. But they were moving very slowly.

"This is very odd," said Principal Egbert to Mr. Timm. "Everyone seems to be limping."

"Strangest thing I've ever seen," said Mr. Timm. "I'd better get Nurse Scappel over here."

Max and Charlie were almost to the finish line.

"I don't think I can make it," said Charlie.

"It's not much farther," said Max.

But Charlie couldn't go another step. She and Max tumbled to the ground a few feet from the finish line.

"Look!" yelled Marie. "They fell down! This is our chance."

"Okay, okay," said Clyde. "If you'll carry me, I'll try to finish."

"Clyde, you're the greatest," said Marie as they struggled to their feet.

"I can't finish," Charlie said to Max as she fell down. "My foot hurts."

"Come on, Charlie!" said Max. "I know you can do it! We're still in front. They're coming, but Marie's almost carrying Clyde."

Clyde and Marie were coming up on them fast.

"It's now or never!" said Max. "In fact, it may be too late already."

Charlie and Max started to get up.

"They're getting up!" said Marie. "We have to stop them!"

"No, we don't!" said Clyde. "We'll be past them by the time they get to their feet!"

"I'm not taking any chances," said Marie. "Let's head straight toward them."

Marie pulled Clyde toward Charlie and Max. They had just stood up when Marie stuck her foot out and tripped Charlie.

Charlie and Max fell to the ground.

Marie dragged Clyde across the finish line.

"I won!" she shouted. "I beat Charlie!"

Charlie and Max rolled over and looked toward the finish line.

"Marie did it to me again," said Charlie.

"Maybe not," said Max. "Mr. Timm and Principal Egbert are talking about something. They don't look happy."

Marie was jumping up and down. "I won! I won! I won!"

"No, you didn't," said Principal Egbert. "Mr. Timm and I both saw you trip Charlie."

"But I didn't do it on purpose!" Marie shouted. "My foot just slipped."

"No," said Principal Egbert. "You tripped Charlie on purpose. I hereby strip you of your ribbon and award it to Charlie and Max."

"But that's not fair!" cried Marie.

Principal Egbert looked sternly at Marie. "I also want to know why Charlie and Clyde were limping during this race. Charlie, what happened to your foot?"

"Marie stepped on it," said Charlie.

"I see," said Mr. Egbert. "And Clyde, what about your foot?"

Marie gave Clyde a mean look.

"Marie stepped on it," said Clyde.

"Marie, you will go with my secretary, Miss Peck. Please hand over the ribbon."

"Marie's in for it now," said Max. "Miss Peck is as mean as they come."

Marie looked down at her ribbon. Slowly, she handed it over to Principal Egbert. He gave the ribbon to Charlie. The kids all cheered.

Charlie felt great, even though her foot still hurt.

Principal Egbert turned to Charlie and Clyde.

"Nurse Scappel is at the first-aid station at the other end of the park. Harry will drive you there. Then you can come back."

Principal Egbert helped Charlie and Clyde get on the bus. Harry closed the door and started the engine.

"I'm proud to know you, little lady," he

said to Charlie. "I wish we had more kids like you in this school."

"Thanks," said Charlie. "But it was your great driving and your siren that saved the day."

"Well, let's just call it a team effort," said Harry.

Charlie closed her eyes and tried to relax. But a cold chill from the window made her open her eyes.

The weather sure has changed fast, she thought. *Brrr.* But when she looked outside, it was still sunny and seemed the same.

"I'm cold," said Clyde.

"So am I," said Charlie. "And it's windy in here."

"That's odd," said Harry. "I closed all the windows after we got back from rescuing the cat."

Charlie looked around. The other windows on the bus were closed. But her window was still open.

Charlie leaned over and tried to close the window. But it didn't budge.

"Stuck!" she groaned. "This window is stuck."

Clyde tried the window, too, but it wouldn't move.

"Harry," said Clyde. "We can't close this window."

Harry eased the bus to a stop and walked back to where Charlie was sitting. He grabbed the window handle and pushed up as hard as he could. Up went the window.

"You see?" he said. "There's nothing to it."

Harry returned to his seat and started up the bus. But the engine made a strange coughing noise, and the whole bus shook.

"This creaky old bus is driving me crazy," barked Harry. "I think it's out to get me."

"Brian Ray thinks the bus is haunted," said Clyde.

"It's not haunted," said Harry. "It's just old."

Harry tried starting the engine again. This time it worked perfectly.

"You see?" said Harry. "It's not haunted. It just needs a little repair work."

Charlie slumped down in her chair and closed her eyes again. Then she felt another cold breeze. She opened her eyes and looked

to see if the window had popped open. But the window was shut tight. And all the other windows were closed.

This is spooky, she thought. *The wind is blowing, but all the windows are closed. Maybe this bus* is *haunted.*

A few minutes later, the bus arrived at the first aid station. Nurse Scappel examined Charlie and Clyde.

"Your feet are slightly swollen and black and blue," she said, "but they're only bruised. You'll be fine in a day or two."

Then Harry drove them back to the picnic.

Charlie was really hungry now.

The picnic was wonderful. There were turkey sandwiches and potato salad and pasta and chocolate cake and cookies that Charlie's mom had baked.

It had turned into "the best Field Day ever" after all. Charlie forgot about the strange wind on the bus. Besides, how could the bus be haunted? It was just a silly idea—*or was it?*